CLYDE the HiPPO

CLYDE LIKES TO RIDE

by Keith Marantz

illustrated by Larissa Marantz

PENGUIN WORKSHOP

W

PENGUIN WORKSHOP

An Imprint of Penguin Random House LLC, New York

Penguin supports copyright. Copyright fuels creativity, encourages diverse voices, promotes free speech, and creates a vibrant culture. Thank you for buying an authorized edition of this book and for complying with copyright laws by not reproducing, scanning, or distributing any part of it in any form without permission. You are supporting writers and allowing Penguin to continue to publish books for every reader.

Text copyright © 2020 by Keith Marantz. Illustrations copyright © 2020 by Larissa Marantz. All rights reserved. Published by Penguin Workshop, an imprint of Penguin Random House LLC, New York. PENGUIN and PENGUIN WORKSHOP are trademarks of Penguin Books Ltd, and the W colophon is a registered trademark of Penguin Random House LLC. Manufactured in China.

Visit us online at www.penguinrandomhouse.com.

Library of Congress Cataloging-in-Publication Data is available upon request.

ISBN 9780593094549 (pbk)   10 9 8 7 6 5 4 3 2 1
ISBN 9780593094556 (hc)   10 9 8 7 6 5 4 3 2 1

To Alek, Kela, and Sasha—our endless
source of inspiration
—KM & LM

This is Clyde.

Clyde likes to ride.

Every morning, he and Orson take his tricycle, Mr. Squeaky, for a spin.

The plastic wheels squeak, but it's still Clyde's favorite way to get around.

One day, Clyde walks inside after his morning ride, and his parents shout, "SURPRISE!"

There is a large wrapped gift in the living room.

Clyde wonders what it could be.

He carefully lifts a piece of tape, then makes a little rip in the paper.

"Just open it!" His father laughs.

Clyde opens the present.

"It's a big-boy bike!" his mom exclaims.

"I see," says Clyde. "It's really nice, but I like my tricycle better. And Amanda's trike will be sad if Mr. Squeaky isn't there when we ride together."

"Well, you're outgrowing Mr. Squeaky, so we thought it was time for something bigger," his dad explains. "Let's take a look at it outside."

The new bike looks *enormous* compared to
Mr. Squeaky.

Clyde wonders if his feet will even reach the pedals. What will he do if they don't?

And if he ever fell, it would be a long way down.

Clyde also worries that his arms may be too short to reach the handlebars.

His dad takes out the pump and begins to put air in the tires.

Clyde does not like the idea that the tires could go flat while he is riding.

"Thanks for the new bike, Dad," he says, "but I'm going to stick with Mr. Squeaky for a while."

Clyde rides Mr. Squeaky in his driveway.

Soon he hears a bell ring.

He sees his friend Amanda, but she's not riding her tricycle.

Amanda is riding a *new* bike!

"Where is Miss Pink Pedals?" Clyde asks.

"I'm too big for her now," Amanda says.
"I graduated to Madame Purple Pedals."

"That's a cool name," says Clyde.

"Thanks," says Amanda. "What's your dad doing over there?"

Clyde looks over at his dad. He has already put training wheels on the new bike. Now he's attaching a kickstand.

Mr. Squeaky never had training wheels or a kickstand.

His new bike looks cooler now. It also looks . . . *safe*.

Clyde looks back
at Amanda.

"That's my new bike,"
Clyde says proudly. "I'm
graduating, too."

All afternoon, Clyde practices riding his new bike.

He learns how to coast,

and how to pedal
backward to stop.

He's a little shaky
at first, but soon he
gets the hang of it.

When he's finally ready, Clyde rides
over to Amanda's house.

"What are you going to name your new bike?" Amanda asks.

"Mr. Squeaky the Second," says Clyde. "It doesn't squeak at all, but that way I'll always remember my trusty old friend."

Clyde likes to ride!